A Dinosaur Called Tiny

For Sarah, who had a big heart,
with much love
—A.D.

To my beautiful Isla and her wonderful dad,
and with love to Mum, Dad, Mark, and Matthew
—J.S.

A Dinosaur Called Tiny
Text copyright © 2007 by Alan Durant
Illustrations copyright © 2007 by Jo Simpson

Manufactured in Singapore.
For information address HarperCollins Children's Books, a division of HarperCollins Publishers,
1350 Avenue of the Americas, New York, NY 10019.

www.harpercollinschildrens.com

Library of Congress Cataloging-in-Publication Data is available.
ISBN 978-0-06-136633-8 (trade bdg.)

Typography by Jeanne L. Hogle

1 2 3 4 5 6 7 8 9 10
❖
First American Edition, 2008
Originally published in Great Britain by HarperCollins Children's Books, 2007

A Dinosaur Called Tiny

by **Alan Durant**

illustrated by **Jo Simpson**

HarperCollins*Publishers*

One sunny day a long, long time ago . . .

crack!

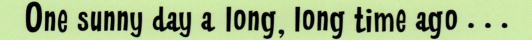

A Dinosaur Called Tiny

by Alan Durant

illustrated by Jo Simpson

HarperCollins*Publishers*

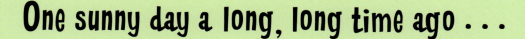

crack!

out of a great, big
dinosaur egg

hatched a little

dinosaur baby.

out of a great, big
dinosaur egg

hatched a little

dinosaur baby.

"Oh, isn't he sweet?" said his mom.
"He's very small," said his dad.
They called him Tiny.

Days, weeks,
months passed.

Tiny grew . . .
a little.

Soon he wasn't a baby anymore,

but he was still tiny.

"He's smaller than one of my spots," said Brontosaurus.

"He's smaller than one of my horns," said Triceratops.

"He's smaller than one of my teeth," said Tyrannosaurus.

No one had ever seen such a tiny dinosaur before.

The other young dinosaurs teased Tiny.
They called him names like Teeny Tiny
and Teensy-Weensy.
"You're not like us," said Tyro,
the young Tyrannosaurus Rex.
"You're much too small."
He stuck out his tongue at Tiny.

Tiny had to play on his own.

At first he tried to copy the games
the other dinosaurs played.

When they played

shake-the-earth . . .

so did Tiny.

But the earth didn't shake at all.

When the other
dinosaurs played
chase-the-dinosaur . . .

Tiny played
chase-the-leaf.
But the leaves never chased him.

"Hello," chirped
a small voice
above him.

Tiny looked up to see a little bird.

"Who are you?" asked Tiny.
"I'm Archie," said the bird.

"I'm Tiny," said Tiny.
"You are," said the bird.

"And you're sad," he added. "Why?"
"No one will play with me." Tiny sighed.
"They say I'm too small."
"I'll play with you," said Archie.
"Because I'm small?" said Tiny.

"No, because I like you," said Archie.

So Tiny and Archie played together.

They played dinosaur's footsteps

and dinosaur explorers. They made a tiny mountain and a little cave.

They had lots of fun.

Suddenly . . . Crash! Crack! Rumble!

The ground shook.

"What was that?" gasped Tiny.

Tiny and Archie went to see.

1

They found the other young dinosaurs in a huddle.
"What's going on?" asked Tiny.
"Tyro jumped so hard, he made the
ground crack," said one dinosaur.
"Now he's trapped," said another.
"And we're scared the ground will break under
us if we try to save him," said a third.

They found the other young dinosaurs in a huddle.
"What's going on?" asked Tiny.
"Tyro jumped so hard, he made the
ground crack," said one dinosaur.
"Now he's trapped," said another.
"And we're scared the ground will break under
us if we try to save him," said a third.

Tiny looked down at his little feet
and thought. "I'll save him," he said,
and off he went.

All around Tiny the ground

creaked

and

crumbled.

Tiny looked down the deep,
dark cracks and shivered.
What if he fell in?

"Help!"
he heard Tyro
cry again.

Tiny had to go on.

On he crept,

and on . . .

. . . until at last he came to where
Tyro stood, shaking and quivering.
"Come on, Tyro," said Tiny. "I'll lead you to safety."
"I c-can't," Tyro sobbed. "I'm s-scared I'll f-fall."

"No, you won't," said Tiny.
"Archie will show us where
it's safe to walk."

"That's right,"
chirped Archie.

Slowly ... but surely,

with Archie's help, Tiny led Tyro ...

... to where the other dinosaurs were waiting.
"Well done, Tiny!" they cried. "You saved Tyro."

"Thanks, Tiny," said Tyro.
He carried Tiny on his back all the way home.

Tiny was a hero.
Now all the dinosaurs
wanted to be friends with him.

No one ever said he was too small or called him Teensy-Weensy again.